FINDING DAVID

A Short Story by
STEVIE TURNER

OTHER WORKS BY STEVIE TURNER

THE PILATES CLASS

A HOUSE WITHOUT WINDOWS

FOR THE SAKE OF A CHILD

LILY: A SHORT STORY

NO SEX PLEASE, I'M MENOPAUSAL!

A RATHER UNUSUAL ROMANCE

THE DAUGHTER-IN-LAW SYNDROME

REVENGE

THE NOISE EFFECT

CRUISING DANGER

THE DONOR

REPENT AT LEISURE

LIFE: 18 SHORT STORIES

ALYS IN HUNGERLAND

MIND GAMES

LEG-LESS AND CHALAZA

PARTNERS IN TIME

CONTENTS

CHAPTER 1 - RAE

She risked a sneaky peep around the curtain; every seat in Croydon's grandly named Athaneum was taken. Desperate for a miracle, rows of overweight middle aged women waited impatiently. A cacophony of chatter filled the air. Women laughed nervously or threw a few words to the odd unsmiling husband sitting in stolid disbelief with arms crossed as if to ward off evil spirits.

The usual high-pitched buzz of anticipation echoed off the walls. Rae Cordelle patted her black bobbed hair into place, stepped back into the wings, and took a deep breath.

"There's a good crowd tonight."

Medicine Horse, six foot seven inches of calm serenity in loincloth and full Apache feathered headdress, emitted a comforting presence as he stood in quiet contemplation by her side.

"I am here to guide you, as always."

Rae gave a nod of approval.

"Many thanks. May God be with us tonight."

Peter Jones, Spiritualist Preacher, raised a water jug towards her in salutation as he slipped through the curtain. All at once Rae heard silence from the discordant hell of many raised voices.

"Ladies and gentlemen, we have a remarkable and gifted clairvoyant medium here with us tonight. I want you to give a big hand to … Rae Cordelle!"

The stagehand pulled back the curtains. Rae, already desperate for the soothing balm of water, walked towards the table to polite applause as the preacher ceased his theatrical posturing and sat down beside her.

"Thank you Peter." She filled a glass and took a refreshing sip. "It's lovely to be here."

Arms folded and his features inscrutable, Medicine Horse stood sentinel at the back of the hall. Rae felt the burning stares of at least two hundred pairs of eyes.

"Has anybody seen me work before?"

A couple of hands shot up while a gabble of deceased spirits jostled for first position in a queue behind Medicine Horse.

"Well, for the others here that haven't attended a demonstration of clairvoyance before, don't worry. If you see anything scary I'll be the first one out of the door, ahead of you all!"

Rae felt the tense atmosphere lighten a fraction, as a titter erupted amongst the cauliflower heads and bald pates. She took another sip of water, and carried on.

"And if your relative was a miserable old bugger in this world, you can bet your bottom dollar he'll be just as miserable in the next!"

Rae perched on the edge of the table until the laughter had ceased.

"I'm clairvoyant. That means I can *see* Spirit." She paused to let the effect of her words sink in. "I first became aware of this gift when I was eight years old. My grandmother came into my room in the middle of the night and woke me up. I thought it strange at the time, because I'd been told she was in hospital over a hundred miles away. She told me she had died, and to let my mother know that she was quite happy and no longer in pain."

Rae looked around the room. Every pair of eyes were fixed upon her.

"I raced into my parents' room shouting out what my grandmother had said. Mum sat up in bed just as the phone rang. It was the night staff at the hospital telling her that her mother had died ten minutes before."

There were a couple of audible gasps. Rae, warmed up, took off her jacket and paced up and down the hall, keeping eye contact with the audience. Heads swung back and forth like a Centre Court crowd at Wimbledon.

"Mother was terrified and wanted to take me to a psychiatrist. Dad told her to let me be. Neither of them ever spoke of it again, but after that incident I saw my grandmother again many times. Other people came to me too – people I'd never seen before."

She had their full attention. Rae nodded at the first one in the queue, then pointed towards an orange aura at the end of the fifth row.

"Can I come to the lady with the blue jacket on please? All you have to do when I come to you is say yes or no."

"Yes."

The reply was barely audible. Rae smiled at the woman and tried to ease her nervousness, which was not helped by the fact that several in the audience had turned in their seats to look.

"I have a lady here – quite tall and willowy, with a hair in some kind of French pleat. She tells you not to worry about your hospital appointment, and that you'll be fine. She's your mother?"

"Y-yes."

The woman's eyes were filling up. Rae decided to change the subject.

"You have an orange aura. I sense you can be a bit hot-headed, but don't hold any grudges, but that you tend to rush into relationships a too quickly."

"Yes!"

The woman nodded and wiped her eyes.

"Your mother sends much love, and tells you that a new man will come into your life next year. You must come back and tell me if he does!"

"Yes." The woman clutched her friend for support. "I will."

"Thank you." Rae mentally beckoned the next one forward. "God be with you."

The woman relaxed into her seat.

"And with you."

Rae smiled, glad of her first success of the evening. She then became aware of a young man aged about 24 or 25, who stood before her, solid and well-built.

"My mum is the lady at the end of the back row with the ginger hair. The man with her is my step-father. I was left for dead when I was nine years old, and my step-father got away with it."

Caught off guard, Rae glanced at Medicine Horse in alarm. The old Indian's healing thoughts immediately permeated her brain.

Say nothing to cause fear. Encourage her to see you after the demonstration ends. The man speaks much truth.

The young man had a slight tic; a twitch of his mouth coupled with frequent sniffs added to an overall feeling of nervousness. Rae noticed a dark grey aura around the stepfather, whose eyes followed her every move.

"Can I come to the lady at the back with the ginger hair?" She walked towards the back of the hall, purposely avoiding any eye contact with the woman's partner. "The lady at the end of the row please."

"Yes."

The woman's son and Medicine Horse stood in close proximity. Rae recited a quick prayer under her breath.

"There's a young man here with me – blond hair and quite handsome. He seems a bit anxious. Do you know who he is?"

Rae noticed a faint smile of recognition.

"Could it be my son David? He was only a child when he went missing though, not a man."

"They grow in the spirit world." Rae replied gently. "Just as our children do here, but they can also present as the child they were if you prefer it."

The woman's features relaxed.

"It's been fifteen years since he went, and I've come to terms with it. I realised a long time ago that he must have died."

The woman's partner shifted slightly in his seat, and Rae ignored the sting of his gaze. The young spirit stood behind his mother and put his arms around her neck and rested his head on her shoulder.

"David is cuddling you." Rae smiled. "He loves you very much."

Rae could hear some of the women sobbing behind her, but the object of her attention remained stoic, lifting up one hand towards her shoulder as if to ruffle her dead son's hair.

"Thank you for your kind words. They mean a lot to me."

"Do take one of my business cards after the demonstration." Rae indicated towards the table at the front of the hall. "I can't spend a lot of time with each person tonight, but if you'd like to call me we could talk some more."

The woman nodded. The next person in the queue made her presence felt, and Rae saw David fade back into the ether.

CHAPTER 2 – KAREN

When Mick sloped off to the toilet she grabbed a business card and made it back to the foyer with minutes to spare. She filtered out the door with the rest of the crowd when she saw him return and rolled her eyes in anticipation of his reaction, which was quick to arrive.

"What a load of bollocks *that* was."

She shook her head.

"I don't think so. It was comforting to me to know that David's still around."

She fastened her jacket against the cold air and enjoyed the warmth of Mick's hand in hers as they strolled towards the car park. She felt him give her fingers a squeeze.

"Don't be taken in by people like that. They're only there to get you to pay out forty quid for a private reading."

She decided there and then not to let him know how she was prepared to work until she dropped to earn whatever it took to be able to communicate with her son again.

"You're probably right." She clutched the business card in her pocket with her free hand. "I suppose they just tell us what we want to hear."

Mick pressed the central locking button on his keyring to open their Ford Kuga.

"Exactly. As I said… it's all a load of old bollocks."

***

Her chance came towards the end of January. She almost pushed Mick out of the door when his monthly darts' evening came around.

"Give me a call if Steve's not bringing you home as well, unless you're on orange juice tonight?"

"Yeah, orange juice all night." He chuckled and kissed her cheek. "See you later."

She waved the two of them off and closed the front door with a sigh of relief before heading straight for her wardrobe and scrutinising the medium's business card as she took it out of her jacket pocket. She flopped down onto the bed, and tapped the number into her mobile phone.

"Hello?"

It was the voice of the clairvoyant. Karen spoke slowly to ensure the whole sorry story didn't tumble out of her mouth like a dose of verbal diarrhoea.

"I'm Karen Curtis. Er…you spoke to me at the Athenaeum about a month ago regarding my son David. You said to ring, and I took one of your cards. I've a feeling you have more to tell me?"

Her heart pounded in her chest. Karen exhaled purposefully, and briefly closed her eyes. When a voice answered after a short pause, the tone was calm and somehow rather soothing.

"I was hoping you'd get in touch. Yes, I'd like to see you again if I may."

Karen remembered Mick's words.

"I'm afraid I can't afford a private reading."

"This will be free. It's on *me*. If we meet, then David will come back. I couldn't tell you all he said at the Athenaeum right at this moment, but it's quite important that you come and see me."

Intrigued, Karen sat bolt upright.

"My husband is out for at least another four hours. Can I come to you right now? Where do you live?"

The address was a short drive away, on the outskirts of South East London. Karen leapt off the bed, phone in hand.

"I'm on my way."

***

The row of terraced houses in Eastleigh Drive looked ordinary enough. Cars were parked either side of a wide avenue fringed with poplar trees, their branches bare of foliage. Karen parked her car and walked along the pavement to number 22 and opened the gate. She was greeted almost at once by the woman she recognised as Rae Cordelle, who threw open her front door somewhat theatrically.

"I'm so glad you could come!"

The greeting seemed genuine. Karen smiled.

"I must say, I'm very intrigued."

"Of course." Rae closed the front door behind her. "But it's not the sort of thing we can talk about in public. Follow me along the passageway here."

Karen found herself ushered into a fairly spacious office, the walls of which were draped with swathes of purple chiffon. Certificates rested in polished frames atop a large Edwardian-type desk on which sat a computer, printer, bulging in-tray, and a cordless phone. Two leather armchairs faced each other either side of a coffee table, which had been placed at the opposite end of the office next to the only window. A small fan heater blasted out unpleasantly hot air in her face. A dog barked from somewhere inside the house.

"Grab an armchair. Would you like some tea or coffee?"

"I'm fine, thanks." Karen shook her head and shifted away from the fan heater. "Thank you for not charging me. Funds are a bit light just after Christmas."

She wished her unruly curls resembled the medium's sleek black bob, who had already made herself comfortable in the other armchair.

"No problem. David is already here with us."

Karen took a sharp intake of breath and forced herself not to scrutinise her surroundings looking for someone that only Rae Cordelle could see. Mick's scepticism suddenly came to the fore.

"Please could you get David to tell me something that only he and I would know."

"Sure." The medium paused for a moment before replying. "David says that when he had chicken-pox, you brought him chocolate button sandwiches in bed."

At those words she wiped away a few tears and glanced in vain about her.

"I did. That's amazing. You're very gifted. I so wish I could see him."

"He knows that." Rae nodded. "But he can see *you*, and he wants you to know something, but it's going to be a great shock to you."

Karen brought her hand up instinctively to her face.

"What?"

"That he was left for dead." Rae replied matter-of-factly. "And his step-father got away with it."

"Murdered by Mick?" Karen, horrified, shook her head. "No, that's not possible!"

Her orderly, conventional world came crashing down around her ears. Karen, immediately frozen in disbelief, wondered whether the medium was crazy.

"Get him to tell me something else."

She only had a few moments to gather her thoughts before another onslaught.

"He says you have a photo of him in a silver frame on a shelf above your TV. Some nights when you sit with your husband watching a programme, he doesn't know that you're really staring at David's face instead."

"Oh God!" Karen cried in anguish. "I can't believe this is happening to me!"

She looked at the medium, who reached across the table and briefly took her hand.

"I can only inform you of what Spirit tell me."

Karen took a tissue from a box on the table and wiped her eyes.

"How?" She sniffed. "How did he do it?"

Rae mumbled thanks to somebody Karen could not see.

"He says that one late afternoon your husband looked after him while you were shopping and then working a night shift at a care home. He tells me your husband kicked him out of the car on Dartmoor and left him there in the snow and ice in temperatures which had dropped to minus ten."

Karen felt sick and put her head in her hands.

"I came home the next morning with David's Christmas present in the car to find the police at our house and no sign of my son. Mick said he'd lost sight of David at a Christmas fair in Okehampton, and that he'd been abducted."

"I'm so sorry." Rae sighed. "But I have to pass on what David tells me. He says his body was eaten by wild animals, and how there was nothing left to find in the spot where he died except for a few bones."

Karen could not stop the tears, which flowed as though burst from a dam that had held them for fifteen long years.

"The police searched for weeks." She sobbed. "Mick helped them, and so did I. We even made the national news!"

"Once again, I'm very sorry." Rae poured some water into a glass and took a sip. "Your son wants justice for his murder."

Karen blew her nose and wiped more tears away.

"But there's no proof! How can I go to the police? They'll laugh at me, or even think *I* killed him if I take them to where David's bones are! Mick's been a fantastic husband all these years. I can't believe he would have done something like this!"

"I think he wanted you all to himself." Rae replied. "David was a thorn in his side that constantly reminded him you had been with another man. If you wish, I could go with you to Dartmoor and David can show us where his remains are."

Karen exhaled a long, shaky breath.

"Ask him if he can do that."

"David's already told me he can find his bones." Rae nodded. "It won't prove who killed him, but it might give you some closure. I already have your mobile number I think. I'll meet you in Ashburton – it's a small town I've been to a few times that's on the edge of Dartmoor. Ring me when you arrive.

"Okay." Karen replied. "Let's do it."

CHAPTER 3 – MICK

Mick Curtis packed away his darts and finished up the dregs from his pint of bitter just as the 'time' bell sounded at the Cat & Fiddle. Behind the counter two bored-looking young barmaids stood glued to their iPhones.

"Twenty years ago, eh? …" Mick indicated in the direction of the bar.

Steve Parsons gave a throaty chuckle.

"Oh yeah. You're all talk, you are. Anyway, Karen soon put you right."

"True. True." Mick swung his jacket over his shoulder. "Karen's the only woman for me. She saved me from an early death, with her broccoli and her tofu burgers."

Steve laughed, then picked his car keys and a little box of darts.

"Come on, Romeo. Time for bed."

"I bet you say that to all the boys." Mick followed Steve to the door and stopped to give the barmaids a wave.

'Night, girls."

There was no reply. Mick shrugged and stepped out into the cool evening air.

"There was a time one of them would have walked out behind me."

He ignored the raised eyebrow of disbelief from his friend, and climbed into the front of the van, sweeping a couple of empty sandwich wrappers onto the floor from the middle seat.

"This van's a disgrace."

Steve shrugged as he started the engine.

"It gets you home though, doesn't it?"

"Yeah, but my jeans'll be covered in shite."

The two men swapped insults and banter for the remainder of the short journey to Crossleys Street. Mick looked out of the window as Steve pulled the van up on the driveway of number 42.

"Karen's already gone to bed by the looks of it."

"No nooky for you then." Steve made a thumbs down gesture. "It'll have to be the old hand job again."

Mick laughed and slid open the passenger door.

"Get stuffed."

"I will." Steve raised his thumb. "Which is more than you'll be doing. See you at work on Monday."

Mick gave a wave as Steve reversed back into the road and drove away, then fumbled with his key in the darkness. The door swung open to an empty unlit hall. Mick checked in the living room that Karen had not gone to sleep in her favourite armchair and left the TV on, then crept upstairs and switched on the landing light. Worried slightly, he popped his head around the bedroom door.

The bed had not been slept in. He noticed their wardrobe door standing ajar, and a space above it where a large suitcase had been. He quickly checked the bathroom and then the spare bedroom, but both were empty. He ran back down the stairs, glanced in the kitchen, dining room, downstairs lavatory, and in the front room again for good measure. Finally he pulled the phone out of his pocket and tapped in the number he knew so well.

"What?"

Karen's voice sounded angry to his ears. Mick thought back through the day and tried to remember if he'd done anything to piss her off.

"Where are you?"

"I'm driving up the M5."

"What the fuck for? It's nearly midnight!"

"Because I feel like it."

He wracked his brain, but the day had been like any other…

"Tell me where you're stopping for the night, and I'll come and find you."

There was no reply and the line went dead. Mick tried three more times to call the number again, but without success. Stressed and puzzled, he flopped down onto the settee and wondered what the hell was wrong with his wife.

***

Promptly at nine o'clock the next morning he picked up the phone and dialled the Autumn Glow Residential Home.

"Yes. Can I help you?"

The female voice sounded overly-authoritative. Mick matched his own tone to the blonde Hitler-ette's, whom he knew Karen hated with a vengeance.

"I'd like to speak to Karen Curtis please."

"She's taken a week's emergency annual leave. She'll be back for an afternoon shift next Saturday. If you leave your name and number, I'll get her to call you when she returns."

Mick slammed the phone down and let out an expletive. *Had she found a new man?* He didn't think Karen had been acting strangely at all, but her disappearance was well out of character. However, if a new man *was* on the scene, Mick was certain of one thing… if *he, Mick,* couldn't have her, then neither would the boyfriend when he found out who the bastard was.

The thought of another man making love to his wife had caused waves of hot anger to wash over him. Mick threw a few things into an overnight bag and scrolled down his phone's contacts until he found the number he was looking for. A voice thick with sleep sounded in his ear.

"Fuck off."

"Steve, it's Mick. Tell Bondy I've had to take some annual leave at short notice. Can't say much at the moment, but it's family problems."

"Okay."

Mick hoped his pal was awake enough to take in what he'd said. He ended the call and made for the front door, grabbing his car keys from the hall table on the way.

CHAPTER 4 – KAREN

Karen looked out of the window of her room on Ashburton's main street. The retro-style town looked to her as though it had been pulled back in time to the 1950s. Antique shops crammed with over-priced goods jostled with a number of quaint tea rooms, art galleries, bookshops and the odd modern-looking supermarket for the attention of the well-to-do.

The town stirred, and shopkeepers unlocked the doors to their emporiums. Turning away from the window, Karen trod carefully down the steep, narrow staircase towards the breakfast room, each step creaking loudly as she did so. A baby cried from somewhere in the distance, and an aroma of frying bacon wafted on the air.

"Good morning!"

The grinning waitress was too jolly for Karen's mood. She smiled, then took a seat at a corner table as far away from anybody else as she could manage. A menu was thrust into her hands.

"Full English or continental?"

"Neither, thanks." Karen shook her head. "Is it possible to have just beans on toast and a cup of tea please?"

The grin faltered a little, before the waitress walked away towards the kitchen. Karen tapped a short message to Rae Cordelle while she waited for her food:

'Just having breakfast at the Olde Tea Room in the High Street. Give me a bell in about half an hour and I'll come straight out.'

***

The weak warmth of the winter sun promised a fine day ahead. Karen gathered her coat and bag, and raised an eyebrow as she peeped through pristine net curtains to see Rae standing on the pavement next to a shiny black Porshe Boxster.

Clairvoyancy pays a bit better than washing arses.

The breakfast room was full as she passed along the hallway and out into the street.

"Hello." Karen smiled at the medium. "Nice car."

Rae smiled and raised her hand in greeting.

"Thanks. It's my husband's. Mine's in for repair."

The seat was lower down than she was used to. Karen saw a couple of youths pass by and give the Porshe a once-over. Rae emitted a low chuckle.

"In their dreams…"

"Rae…" Karen turned towards Rae, who had started up the engine. "I think we'd better get the police involved in this. Do you agree?"

"Sure." The medium nodded. "I had the same idea. Google the local police station and we'll go there first, if you like."

With some reluctance Karen switched on her mobile phone to find 15 text messages and 10 missed calls.

"Here's the postcode for the satnav." She held the screen towards Rae. "My husband's desperately trying to contact me. I'd rather turn my phone off again until we've finished what we came here to do."

"Okay. Let's get going and see what the day brings. I've got some shovels in the boot, just in case."

***

Karen felt shaky with nerves as she faced the desk sergeant.

"I have with me Mrs Rae Cordelle, a medium who says she can shed new light on my son David Nelson's disappearance."

"Is that so?" The burly sergeant looked unconvinced. "How's that, then?"

She ignored the veiled sarcasm and continued.

"Mrs Cordelle can take us to the spot on Dartmoor where he died, back in two thousand and four. I assume you still have an open case on him? He vanished after a day out with his stepfather at Okehampton's Christmas Fair."

"If you two ladies would care to take a seat, I'll have a look back through our files and see what we've got. But if you're not familiar with the area, the moorland covers over three hundred and fifty miles, and it's not exactly summer out there. You can go to the exact place?"

"Yes." Rae nodded. "I have my spirit guide with me."

"And we lived in Devon for some years when David's stepfather and I were first married. We moved to London due to my husband's new job." Karen disliked the sergeant already. "David's father still lives near Exeter, so I already know how many miles are involved."

The sergeant disappeared with a faint snort of disapproval. Sighing, Karen flopped down into the first vacant chair she saw. Rae put on her glasses to fathom the workings of the coffee machine.

"Want one?"

"No thanks." Karen shook her head. "I've got the jitters enough as it is."

The sergeant returned carrying a buff folder, and with a forefinger beckoned the women forward.

"I see David went missing on December the eighteenth two thousand and four."

Karen craned her neck to read the file.

"Yes, this coming December will be fifteen years since I last saw him. Your colleagues at the time organised a massive search, but he was never found. We appeared on TV too. The BBC received three hundred phone calls of sightings which were all checked out, but none were any good."

The sergeant turned towards Rae.

"What makes you think you know any better?"

Karen felt the antipathy rising, and wanted to punch the smug sergeant in the face.

"David came to me as a spirit entity." Rae explained as though to a child. "As long as his mother is with me, then the love between them ensures that David is here too. Can you not see him?"

Karen suppressed a grin.

"'Fraid not." The sergeant replied testily. "I deal with what I can see, not what I can't."

Rae sniffed.

"Then I'm sorry for you. Can we get on with this? Would you be able to send an officer with us to verify any findings?"

"We don't sit around all day waiting for the chance to go ghost-hunting." The sergeant snapped the file shut. "The officers are all out at the moment."

"Standing behind trees with speed guns?" Karen ventured with an icy smile. "Come on, Rae. Let's sort it out on our own."

"Good idea." Rae nodded towards the sergeant. "By the way, your grandmother is standing next to you. She says the lock is stiff to your front door at home, and you have trouble inserting the key. Don't worry, she tells me you'll never have any more problems opening the door again."

With the sergeant's mouth open in an 'o' of surprise, Rae turned on her heel and walked out of the door.

CHAPTER 5 – KAREN

Karen closed the door of the Porshe with perhaps rather more force than was necessary.

"What an absolute *pig* of a man!"

Rae started up the engine and fastened her seat belt.

"Don't let him get to you. There's a whole other world out there that he'll never see, because like a lot of men he wants proof. These people reject everything and anything they cannot see with their own two eyes."

"*I* believe in you, anyway." Karen exhaled a calming breath. "How *could* you have known about the photo of David above the TV and the chocolate button sandwiches? We'd never met before!"

"Exactly." Rae slipped into first gear and pulled away from the kerb. "It's no use trying to convince him. He'll have a think about what his grandmother said, go home and open the door quite easily, but then put it all down to WD40 and coincidence."

Karen chuckled.

"Where's David now?"

Rae took the slip road.

"Sitting on your side of the bonnet letting the wind whip through his hair."

Karen looked through the front windscreen at the Devon Expressway.

"I *so* wish I could see him. You have a wonderful gift."

"I didn't ask for it." Rae replied. "It found *me*. Karen…Medicine Horse is showing me two bridges. Sorry to ask you to turn your phone on again, but could you check whether there's a road called Two Bridges nearby on Google, please?"

With some reluctance, Karen took the iPhone from her bag. She ignored a further three incoming text messages as she called up the search engine.

"Yes. There's a Two Bridges Road on Dartmoor, the B3212, near the Fox Tor Café. I've got the postcode for the café. I'll tap it into your satnav."

"Great." Rae turned to grin at Karen.

"And it's got a bunkhouse for us to stay overnight, cycles for hire, and they even sell thermal underwear!"

Rae muttered a few words under her breath.

"I'm just saying thanks to Medicine Horse. Hopefully we won't need to stay overnight, but we might need the thermal underwear."

Karen imagined the café as a beacon of light in the middle of Dartmoor, but was quite surprised to find it standing solid as a rock along Princetown's village street just like any other. She stepped out of the Porsche and noticed groups of hikers already walking towards the miles of empty open moorland. She shivered as a cold wind whipped through her coat.

"At least we won't be on our own."

"Of course not." Rae locked the car. "We've got David and Medicine Horse with us. They say we'll need mountain bikes though."

"Oh God." Karen put a hand to her mouth. "I haven't ridden a bike in years!"

"You never forget, apparently. Methinks I'm going to need to buy some warmer clothes."

Karen nodded.

"Me too."

***

They had only ridden a short distance and already the muscles in her legs were complaining. With one hand Karen pulled her hat further over her forehead as the unfamiliar rucksack bounced around on her back over the rutted ground.

"I'm not used to this."

"Me neither." Rae puffed, slightly out of breath. "It'll be a great ride back down though. David is leading us further up this hill, then we have to walk across the moorland a bit, to the spot where wild horses stand by a tor. He says there was freezing fog when he was left to fend for himself, and he couldn't see too far into the distance."

Fuelled with anger, Karen turned the pedals faster.

"Poor little mite. I don't know how anybody could do that to a child."

Rae stopped the bike and took a bottle of water out of its holder on the crossbar.

"David says that death came quickly, as he was only clad in his football shorts and tee shirt in freezing temperatures. He'd had a coat on at the fair, but he says that Mick took it away."

Karen was glad of the rest. She took a sip of water, unsure whether her eyes were watering due to the wind, or because of the mental image of her son wandering unforgiving moorland in the depths of winter whilst calling her name in vain.

She applied force to the pedals with renewed vigour until Rae held out one hand and slowed down about 15 minutes later.

"We'll have to push the bikes from here. Going over the moorland will be a bit bouncy."

Her legs ached terribly, and she wanted the whole ordeal to be over. Karen dismounted, sweating in the chilly air but glad of no more hills to climb as she traipsed behind Rae over rough, pitted ground.

"How much longer? My legs are like jelly."

Rae turned to look over her shoulder.

"See that tor in the distance? David says his bones have been buried near there by a fox. I've got a little trowel in my rucksack. Did you bring one?"

Karen looked towards the horizon, where the outline of two wild horses grazed by a solid edifice measuring about ten feet in height.

"Yes." She panted. "But at least they won't be buried too deep if it's a fox."

She plodded on, not really taking in the beauty of the countryside. In front, Rae conversed quietly with David and Medicine Horse. Karen felt a twinge of excitement as the tor grew ever nearer.

CHAPTER 6 – MICK

Mick paced the confines of his Travelodge room. The day was half over and still no phone call. The maids were itching to open the door and although he needed to check out, he had no idea where to go next. He swore under his breath as he heard a gentle tap at the door.

"Give me five minutes and then I'll be ready to go!"

He swung his bag over one shoulder and tried her number again. To his surprise, it rang.

"What?"

Her voice sounded cold and distant. Mick spoke quickly, heart beating fast and with an urgent need to be heard.

"Can we meet? Where are you? I don't know what I've done! I'm at Exeter Services. Are you nearby?"

"Me and Rae are on our way to Ashburton Police Station."

"Who's Ray?" His anger began to rise again. "Where did you meet him?"

"R-A-E. She's female. For your information I've got David's leg bone in a plastic bag."

"What the hell…?"

Hearing further knocking he stomped over to the door, threw it open with force, and strode down the corridor past the maids with his phone clamped to one ear.

"Karen… will you tell me what's going on?"

The voice that replied was calm and without emotion.

"I'm going to tell the police how you left my son to die on Dartmoor in the depths of winter."

The conversation ended abruptly. Mick slung his room key at the reception desk and tried without success to redial the number. He gave up on the third attempt and ran to his car. With trembling fingers he tapped in the station's postcode on his satnav, started up the engine, and screeched out of the car park.

***

"I want to see my wife."

The desk sergeant looked up from his paperwork.

"And who might *she* be, may I ask?"

Mick's fingers balled into fists by his sides and he took a deep breath.

"Karen Curtis. She told me she was coming here."

"Oh yes. Mrs Curtis." The sergeant sighed, slightly irritated. "She's in the interview room with her friend. Follow me and you can see her."

"Hang on a minute, mate. I'd like to see my wife alone, without the friend there."

The sergeant nodded while walking along a corridor behind the counter. Mick found himself ushered into a small room at the end.

"Sit here in here and I'll bring her. You and your wife will need to stay nearby until we get the results of the DNA tests."

Mick looked around for a two-way mirror and then up at the ceiling for a camera. Spotting both, he sat down in a chair and closed his eyes, readying himself for the upcoming meeting.

Suspicious and unsmiling, his wife appeared behind another detective, whom Mick supposed would go straight to the two-way mirror after closing the door.

"Hello Karen."

There was no reply. He smiled at her, but her features remained impassive as she took a seat at a small table opposite him. He cleared his throat in preparation for launching a counter attack.

"So you think I've murdered David?"

"Yes." She fixed him with an icy stare. "It would appear so."

"What proof have you got?" Animated, he sat forward on his seat. "I told you at the time, he went missing at the Christmas fair. I took my eyes off him for a minute or two to look at something. When I turned around he was gone."

He watched her, hawk-like, as she shook her head.

"David visited Rae Cordelle on the night we went to see her at the village hall. He told her what really happened – how you drove him out to Dartmoor in mid-December and left him there in thin clothing that was no protection from the ice and snow. David and Rae led me to the spot on the moors where he died, and we found a bone. It's being tested now for DNA, and if it matches mine, that's proof enough."

Mick stood up and began to pace up and down.

"*Somebody* drove him there, sure, but not me. I was at the fair looking everywhere for him! You can ask whichever police were there at the time, if you can find them. We searched together for a good three hours."

"You're a bloody liar!" Karen banged her fist on the table. "Rae is a genuine medium, one of the few about. She's told me things that proves this. How the hell would she know I gave David chocolate button sandwiches when he had chicken pox, and that there's a photo of him on a shelf above our TV?"

Mick shrugged.

"She's guessing. They all do that – and prey on grieving women who'll believe anything they say."

"Well, I *do* believe her." Karen let out a sigh of exasperation. "She's given me the proof I want."

Mick stopped pacing and sat down.

"And you believe *her* instead of me?" He faced Karen and shook his head. "What kind of wife are you?"

She met his look of undisguised hatred with one of her own

"An angry one."

CHAPTER 7 – KAREN

The guest house owner rapping on her door at 6 o'clock in the morning was never a good indication of things to come. Karen yawned, climbed out of bed, and wrapped a robe around her whilst stumbling towards the din. She turned the key and came face to face with a six foot four inch wall of stone.

"Mrs Karen Curtis?"

Karen saw the landlady hovering in the background, still clad in her nightwear. She nodded.

"Yes, that's me."

"I'm Detective Inspector Richardson. I'm arresting you for the murder of David Michael Nelson on or around the date of December the eighteenth two thousand and four. You do not have to say anything, but it may harm your defence if you do not mention when questioned something which you later rely on in court. Anything you do say may be given in evidence."

For a moment she wasn't sure if she had heard him right. She stared at the officer slightly perplexed and open mouthed.

"You think I murdered my own son?"

"Please get dressed as soon as possible." The policeman's features remained impassive. "I will wait here."

Heart pounding in her chest and with no way out save jumping out the upstairs window, she closed the door and looked wildly around the room at her belongings strewn about on various surfaces. Karen had the quickest wash she had ever had, then grabbed any spare clothes and possessions and stuffed them into her rucksack with a sinking feeling of foreboding.

Stonewall stood solid as a rock blocking her escape.

"Come with me please."

"What about my money?" The landlady hopped from foot to foot down by the front door. "She owes me two hundred and eight pounds fifty!"

***

Cold and hungry, she found herself back in the same interview room facing DI Richardson, who switched on a recording device.

"This is eight a.m on the morning of February the fourth, two thousand and nineteen. DI Ken Richardson interviewing Karen Curtis."

Karen's mouth was dry with nerves. She cleared her throat and felt like retching. Her voice, when she spoke, sounded croaky.

"Can I have a cup of tea please?"

"It's on the way." DI Richardson sat forward in his chair, elbows resting on the table. "So… let's begin. Where were you on December the eighteenth two thousand and four - the night your son went missing?"

"At work. You would be able to check with my old employers if you like. I worked a night shift from six p.m to six a.m."

With some relief she saw a uniformed officer enter carrying a tray. Not caring if the tea was scalding hot, she gulped down a mouthful as soon as a cup was set in front of her.

"Thank you." She sighed.

DI Richardson tapped a pen against the edge of the table.

"So… your husband had charge of your son?"

"Yes." Karen nodded and took another sip of tea. "He took him to a Christmas fair at Okehampton so that I could sleep during the afternoon. He phoned me at work around ten p. m to say that David had gone missing and that he and some officers from Okehampton had been searching the area. The search had been called off, but would resume the next day. David was never found. I couldn't leave work as I was the only staff member on duty. It was a terrible night."

She shuddered at the memory, while DI Richardson opened up a file and scanned the first page.

"The DNA from the femur you found is a match for the DNA on the swab we took from the inside of your mouth. Therefore the leg bone *is* David's. Are you going to tell me how you were able to go to the exact spot in the middle of three hundred miles of moorland and dig it up if you hadn't put his body there in the first place?"

Karen looked at the officer in horror.

"If you think I murdered my son, you're mistaken! He was alive when I kissed him goodbye around one o'clock that afternoon. I've had help in finding him from Rae Cordelle, a very gifted medium who was guided there by David himself."

A faint snort of disbelief reached her ears. Nevertheless, she carried on.

"You need to speak to Mrs Cordelle. She'll be able to convince you of her talents. It's quite amazing what she can do."

"Is that so?" DI Richardson's features reflected complete disinterest. "Unfortunately I don't usually put much stock by spirits and ghosts. I tend to rely on what I can see with my own eyes."

"All I can tell you is that no way would I ever have murdered David." Karen shook her head to emphasise the point. "Perhaps you need to be a bit more broadminded and interview Mrs Cordelle. Anyway…why would I come to you with David's leg bone if I *had* murdered him? It doesn't make sense to me. Does it to you?"

The detective shrugged.

"When you're in my line of work, nothing surprises you anymore. What we'll do is this; *you* get on to your old employers and ask them to provide us with proof that you were at work on the night your son went missing, and we'll interview Mrs Cordelle and also your husband. In the meantime, you can go home and go back to work, but stay close to the phone. We'll release you under investigation until more evidence can be unearthed. Leave all your contact details at the desk."

Karen stifled a sigh of relief.

"Will do."

CHAPTER 8 – RAE

She hated the self-righteous prig on sight. Rae folded her arms and stared at DI Richardson across the cheap Formica table.

"I knew where to dig because David himself was telling me."

His sigh of annoyance grated on her ears.

"You'll have to do better than that. Did you and Mick Curtis conspire to kill David Nelson?"

She paused momentarily as Medicine Horse appeared in her peripheral vision. In his arms he held a chuckling three year old girl with curly blonde hair. The girl pointed in the direction of DI Richardson.

"My daddy."

Rae gave silent thanks to Medicine Horse, who bowed his head in acknowledgement.

"Your daughter is here. She's about three years old and has lovely blonde hair, which is curly and in ringlets. She's standing right behind you."

The effect of her words on the officer was instantaneous. DI Richardson, face suddenly pale with fright, lurched around in his chair as though hit with a bolt of lightning.

"What did you say?"

Rae looked above the officer's head, smiled at the infant, and silently asked her name.

"I *said* … that your daughter is right behind you. She tells me her name is Carrie."

DI Richardson, open-mouthed, swung slowly back in his seat. Rae wanted to laugh at the incredulous expression on his face.

"How are you doing this? I can't see *anything* behind me! I've never told any of my colleagues here about Carrie. She was the eldest of my four children, and died of meningitis twenty years' ago."

"I'm a medium." Rae sighed with exasperation. "I see people who have died. They come to me via Medicine Horse, my Red Indian spirit guide. Medicine Horse brought David to me in a demonstration of clairvoyance I did recently. His mother was in the audience, and the love link between them is still strong. David told me his step-father purposely left him for dead on Dartmoor in the depths of winter, and so it's my opinion you should be questioning Karen's husband … not me. David led me to where a fox had buried his bones."

She sat in silence as the officer tried to regain some composure. Presently he closed his file and cleared his throat.

"Tell me something else about Carrie."

Rae looked up at the child, quite content in Medicine Horse's arms. Carrie lifted her right arm and waved a soft toy.

"She's holding a furry light brown teddy bear that's dressed in blue and white stripy dungarees. She says his name is Thaddy."

DI Richardson wiped his eyes.

"We put Thaddy in her coffin with her. She carried him everywhere."

Rae could not help the small self-satisfied smile that briefly softened her features.

"She's out of suffering and has grown up in Spirit, although she comes back to you as the three year old child that you remember. Your mother raised her to adulthood by the way."

The officer, by now barely able to contain his emotions, nodded as he exhaled shakily.

"Mum died quite young. Dad brought me and my brother up."

"Can I go now?" Rae stood up. "I take it I've given you enough proof of my innocence?"

DI Richardson rose to his feet, right arm outstretched.

"Thank you for coming in, and for telling me about Carrie. My wife will be absolutely gobsmacked."

Rae shook the proffered hand.

"Good luck with getting a confession out of Mick Curtis."

"Leave that to us." DI Richardson moved towards the door, and opened it. "We may call upon your services again in the near future."

"Any time." Rae gave the officer a smile. "Perhaps you and your wife might like to come along to one of my demonstrations of clairvoyance? All my dates for the next year are on my website. Just Google my name."

"Yes. We sure would."

Rae nodded, then sailed victoriously out of the door

CHAPTER 9 - MICK

Mick tried but failed miserably to banish the mental picture of a cold prison cell from his mind as he sat before DI Richardson the following day. All the odds were stacked against him, and he had a sinking feeling his version of events had not impressed the policeman at all.

"So…" DI Richardson sat back in his chair.

Mick folded his arms and met the officer's stare.

"So?"

DI Richardson stood up.

"At the moment there is insufficient evidence to charge you with the murder of your stepson. What I'm going to do is release you under investigation, as per the Policing and Crime Act of twenty seventeen. You can go home, but be prepared to be called in for another interview at any time, or be formally charged and be remanded in custody until a trial, or even be informed that no further action will be taken. Leave any addresses and telephone numbers where you'll be at the desk, and in the meantime I suggest you seek out a good criminal defence solicitor as well."

Mick felt like leaping for joy as the voice recorder was turned off. However, he kept a tight control of his emotions as he got to his feet.

"Cheers."

Never had he appreciated sunshine more as he walked out of the interview room and into the fresh air. He grabbed the phone from his pocket and tapped in the number he knew so well.

"What?"

"They've let me go under investigation. Load of bollocks. I'm coming home. We'll talk later."

Without waiting for her reply, he ended the call.

***

He could see her car on the driveway as he pulled up outside the house. Mick sighed and briefly slumped back against the head-rest and closed his eyes. Before he knew it he was woken from a brief doze by a tapping at the window and a shrill voice in his ear.

"You don't think you're staying *here*, do you?"

He opened the driver's door and stepped out, facing a furious face of pure hatred.

"Where else is there to go? If you remember rightly I'm the one paying the bloody mortgage on this place, so I've every right to be here!"

He grabbed his bag from the back seat, locked the car and made towards the house, taking advantage of her silence. The door slammed behind him, and he turned around to face his wife, glad to be out of view of twitching curtains.

"Once again, just for the record. I did *not* leave Davy in the middle of Dartmoor. I love you, for Christ's sake… I'd never do that! No man in his right mind would kill the child of a woman he loves. You're an intelligent lady…surely you don't suspect me of murder?"

He walked into the living room and flopped into his armchair, not waiting for her reply. She stormed in and stood in front of him, hands on hips.

"You never liked him! Go on… admit it!"

He shrugged.

"Okay, he got on my tits. That's what kids do…they get on your tits! But I never *ever* laid a hand on him and certainly never left him to die! What do you think I am…some kind of monster?"

"I don't know *what* you are anymore!" Karen wailed. "The rug's been pulled out from under my feet!"

He looked up at her.

"Trust me. Listen…I took him to Okehampton Fair. It was getting dark when I queued up to take Davy on the ghost train. He was standing next to me. As you know… as *everybody* knows…I chatted to the guy in the ticket office because he was in my darts team. After I paid, I looked round for Davy, but he'd gone."

Like a burst balloon, her anger deflated. Devoid of emotion, she sat down.

"I know the guy was interviewed by police at the time. He always said he didn't see anything."

Mick sat forward in his seat.

"Yeah, because he was too up high in the ticket booth. He would have had to look out the front window and downwards to see anything. All he could see was my head. I don't suppose he *would've* seen Davy as he wasn't tall enough, but just because he didn't see anything it doesn't mean I'm lying."

"I don't know what to believe." Karen sighed. "All these years and never a cross word between us. *Now* look at us."

Mick, now in a calmer frame of mind, leaned back and rested his head.

"I'll take the spare room for now. Just have a think about what I've said."

CHAPTER 10 – KAREN

Try as she might, sleep eluded her. Karen lay wide awake while the rest of the world slept, and wondered whether her husband could have really done something so wicked as to leave a child to die. She knew he had always resented the fact that she had been with another man, and David had been proof of that. However, as far back as she could remember, Mick would usually leave punishing the boy to her and had never laid a finger on him.

Tossing and turning had made her hot and sweaty, and she needed a drink. Karen threw back the duvet, climbed out of bed, and put on her robe and slippers. Outside on the landing there were no sounds from the spare room, and as she padded down the stairs she imagined her husband lying there in a similar state of wretched insomnia.

She blinked as the fluorescent bulb in the kitchen spluttered to life. She filled the kettle and switched it on, then slumped onto one of the breakfast bar stools and put her head in her hands.

"Can I have one as well? If it's any consolation, I can't sleep either."

Startled, she sat up and looked around. Mick, clad only in pyjama bottoms, stood in the doorway with his hair standing on end. She nodded and indicated with one hand in the direction of the fridge.

"You get the milk then, as you're up."

She watched him take a half empty milk bottle from the fridge door and then close it. Such a normal action the last time she had seen him do it, but now so much had happened in a short space of time. Karen took the milk from his hand.

"Did you *ever* hit him?"

Mick shook his head.

"You know the answer to that. He didn't like me much… I could tell, but I tried my best with him. Anyway, he wasn't a naughty kid – just irritating sometimes with his constant questions."

Karen nodded.

"He was intelligent. What do you expect with his dad being a university lecturer? David took after him."

"And I'm only a grubby electrician?" Mick's mouth formed a sneer. "Go on, say it … you know you want to. Bet the bastard couldn't have wired up your house though."

Karen sighed.

"I was going to say nothing of the sort. Stop putting words into my mouth. Here's your tea." She handed him a steaming mug. "If you've got an inferiority complex, it's not my fault. Andrew went off with one of his colleagues, as you know. It should be *me* who still has the inferiority complex, but hey, I got over it."

Mick took a noisy gulp of tea and perched on an empty stool.

"Perhaps you might feel differently if everyone's accusing you of child neglect or even murder."

"They already have." Karen's eyes glittered with anger. "The police asked me how I knew where he was buried, so you're not the only one under investigation here."

Mick stood up and made for the door.

"Perhaps *you* did him in then?"

She felt like throwing her mug of tea at his retreating back.

***

The aroma of frying bacon had brought him downstairs, and by the look of him Karen guessed her husband hadn't slept at all.

"Is there any for me, or are you only cooking for yourself now?"

His tone was already belligerent. Karen kept her back to him and held up a large packet of rashers.

"There's plenty for you if you want some."

He gave an audible sigh.

"Cheers."

Her thoughts flew back to the three of them sitting around the breakfast table on Saturday mornings. David would wolf down two bacon rolls, enjoying the wind-up as Mick waited impatiently; the smell of bacon making his mouth water. She knew he would complain at being served after a child, but her brief moment of control was somehow enjoyable.

Karen transferred three sizzling rashers to a plate, added two dry rolls, then slid the plate under Mick's nose.

"Butter's still in the fridge."

She took three more rashers out of the packet and laid them in the frying pan, watching the edges crinkle in the heat. After some moments of silence, she voiced a question that had been on her mind.

"What do we do now then?"

The sound of chewing came from behind. She always hated it when he would speak with his mouth full. As if he knew her very thoughts, he remained silent until every morsel had been eaten.

"God knows. Wait for the police to get in touch, I suppose."

"I didn't kill David." She stabbed at her bacon in the pan. "You must know that."

He shrugged.

"Neither did I, despite what that medium said."

She removed her cooked rashers and put them inside two buttered rolls, then added a generous helping of tomato sauce. She stood by the cooker and ate, keeping her distance.

"David told her himself that you'd left him on the moor."

Mick's chair scraping against the lino jangled her nerves. He stormed towards the cooker, his six-foot frame towering menacingly over her. Karen chewed quietly and stood her ground.

"You believe that woman instead of *me?*"

There was a remnant of bacon at the corner of his mouth. In the past she would have reached up and removed it, but now all she could do was step back against the wall.

"I don't know what to believe."

He snorted in disgust, then turned and walked away. Karen sighed and took another bite of her bacon roll. Rae was a gifted and genuine medium, and Karen knew her new friend was not in the habit of making mistakes. *David had named his murderer from beyond the grave.* How could any mother live with the person who had murdered her child? Karen shook her head and wondered if Autumn Glow's guest room was still empty and available for renting.

CHAPTER 11 – MICK

"Alright mate?"

Mick flopped down in the passenger seat of Steve's van and slammed the door.

"Not really. Sorry we lost tonight. It was all my fault."

Steve turned a key in the ignition, and the engine fired after a couple of tries.

"What's up?"

Mick shrugged.

"Oh, this and that. Try being accused of murder, and then see how many bullseyes *you* can score."

"Eh?" Steve looked around in surprise. "Who have you done in then?"

"That's the point." Mick sighed. "I haven't killed anybody. I might have wanted to bump off a few arseholes over the years, but I value my freedom too much."

Steve engaged first gear and the van rattled off past the Cat & Fiddle.

"Sounds like you might need to get lawyered up? My brother-in-law can help in that department."

"Nah." Mick shook his head. "Let them search for evidence until hell freezes over. All I'm more interested in is convincing Karen."

Steve applied the handbrake at a red light and turned to Mick.

"Trouble on the home front?"

Mick yawned.

"You could say that. Seems I'm up shit creek and some bastard's nicked my paddle."

"I've got a really good sofa at home." Steve briefly turned to Mick before pulling away from the lights. "Reclining seats. It's all yours if you're drowning in the brown stuff."

"Cheers." Mick gave a wry laugh. "I might have to take you up on that."

***

Her shift should have finished by now, but her car was missing. Mick, with a sense of foreboding, gave Steve a farewell wave as the van backed down the driveway and into the road. No lights illuminated the bay window as he walked up the path towards the front door. Inside, the house was quiet and in total darkness.

He reached along the wall and flicked a switch. The first thing he saw was an envelope on the bottom step addressed to him in his wife's handwriting. Trying to ignore his thudding heart, Mick opened the flap and took out the one piece of notepaper hidden inside. What he read disturbed him greatly:

'They're letting me rent the guest room at Autumn Glow, and I'll be staying there for the time being until the police come up with something. I can get subsidised meals at work. Karen.'

None of her usual kisses. He'd just received his first 'Dear John' letter, and it hurt like hell. Mick, with the note screwed up in his fist, punched the unyielding wall with considerable force and then flung the ball of paper as far as he could along the hallway. Taking the stairs two at a time, he ran breathless into their bedroom. Her wardrobe door was slightly ajar and revealed many empty hangers.

Mick slumped down onto the bed. The knuckles of his right hand throbbed, along with a pulse in his head. *How could their previously happy marriage have deteriorated in such a short space of time?* He knew the answer; *it was all that bloody medium's fault!*

He leaped up from the bed and ran into the spare room where the computer sat silently waiting for his fingers to bring it to life. Mick hopped from foot to foot until Google flashed up and then typed in 'Rae Cordelle', grimacing as the woman's sickly smile filled the screen. He sought out the contact page, purposely ignored a box for his email address, and added his mobile phone number instead.

'Hi, I'm John Lucas. I'd like a reading please. Evenings or this weekend if possible.'

A text had arrived by the time he awoke the following morning after his usual Saturday lie-in, and Mick agreed an appointment date for 4pm that afternoon after checking out the medium's address on Google Maps.

***

A low growl followed by formidable barking and a scraping of paws could be heard on the other side of the door. Mick stepped back as a key turned in the lock and a female voice gave a shout.

"Shut up!"

Straight away her features changed as she recognised him. The Alsatian bared his teeth and strained to break free from the hand that held his collar.

"I don't think you're supposed to be here."

Mick shrugged.

"I wanted to speak to you, and I knew you wouldn't see me if I gave my real name."

"What do you want from me?" Rae Cordelle sighed. "Max doesn't like you much, by the way."

Mick took another step back, and removed two twenty pound notes from his wallet.

"I don't go a bundle on him either. I want a reading, like everyone else who comes here. Here - I've got your forty quid."

He saw her eyes quickly focus on the money.

"You'd better come in then. Max will sit with me."

"Fine." Mick stared at the dog's black eyes. "Just as long as he's had his dinner."

A male voice sounded from somewhere in the house.

"Who's that?"

"Someone who's come for a reading!" Rae shouted. "I'll be in the office!"

Mick followed the medium along a passageway, wrinkling his nose at the sudden sight of purple chiffon shrouding all four office walls. He sat in one of the armchairs, keeping a wary eye on the Alsatian, who lay down next to Rae and regarded him with an unblinking hostile stare. Rae crossed her legs and patted the dog's head.

"Would you like tea or coffee?"

"No thanks." Mick shook his head. "Some of that water there would be great."

Rae filled two glasses and pushed one of them in Mick's direction.

"I've got your mother here."

All of Mick's suspicions had been substantiated in those few words. He gave a self-satisfied smile.

"That can't be. My mother is still alive. You're full of shit."

A clock ticked in the background. The dog yawned, and Mick decided to avoid Rae's glittering eyes. However, try as he might, he could not ignore the voice.

"Not the one who adopted you. I'm talking about Rose, your birth mother."

A flashback seared painfully through his mind: A five year old boy trying to wake a woman covered in vomit and surrounded by empty bottles, and the smell that put him off whisky for life. He reluctantly came back to the present and shifted uncomfortably.

"You what?"

"She's sorry for treating you so terribly, and for finding her dead on the settee like you did. She apologises profusely for having no control over her addiction. She loved you. She says you were the only good thing in her life."

Max snored on gently. Rae took a sip of water, and Mick concentrated on rubbing his hands together; trying to wash away thoughts he'd kept hidden for so long.

"You're fucking good, I'll give you that. Where did you find this out? Who told you?"

An audible sigh reached his ears.

"My spirit guide, Medicine Horse, stands next to me. It is *he* who lets the right people through. Without him I would have about as much insight into the spirit world as you obviously do."

The schoolmarm tone to her voice pissed him off more than his mother's excuses. Mick stood up and rubbed his eyes.

"Sorry. I think I've heard enough. I'll see myself out."

The dog was up on all fours in no time. Rae nodded and kept a hand on Max's collar.

"You've paid for another half an hour. Come back again when you've got your head around what I've told you."

He stumbled along the passageway and out into the open air. When seated in the privacy of his car he put his head down and cried hot tears of shame.

CHAPTER 12 – KAREN

It felt strange waking to the sounds of the night shift girls going about their business. Karen sat up and tried not to think of the cup of tea that would normally be on its way to her. Now she would have to make her own.

She threw back the duvet and padded over to the kettle. Living in one room with its en-suite shower was beginning to feel rather claustrophobic and not as exciting as she'd first thought. Most of her clothes were still back at the house, and one half of the old Fifties' style wardrobe in the guest room still stood empty.

With the hot liquid warming her body, Karen looked out of the window. Walter Tomkins wobbled along on his walker towards the shop for his morning newspaper, and the reserved spot in the car park for ambulances was thankfully empty. Nobody needed the paramedics, therefore everything should be well in her world. However, it wasn't. Her marriage was on the rocks, and her husband seemed to be giving the infamous moors' murderers a run for their money.

As she donned her care assistant's uniform, Karen decided to pay another visit to Rae to see whether David still stood by his accusation. She knew in her heart of hearts that Mick was not the type to let a young boy freeze to death, but she realised she would gain more sleep at night if she could hear the reality of it again from her own son's lips.

***

She stepped back down the path as Max gave her the once over.

"Is he okay with me?"

"Come in." Rae laughed. "You would have found out by now if he wasn't."

Karen entered the now familiar purple office, sat down in the same armchair as before, and took out her purse. Max headed to his basket.

"No, it's on me." Rae shook her head. "I'm just happy to help. Tea or coffee before we start?"

"Water, thanks. You're very kind."

She took a sip from the proffered glass, almost choking at the medium's next words.

"Your husband was in here the other day."

"What!" Karen coughed. "He actually wanted a reading?"

"He did, but what I said scared him off I think. He only stayed about ten minutes."

Karen sat forward in her seat.

"What did you tell him? Did he want to speak to David?"

"I'm afraid I can't tell you due to confidentiality issues." Rae shrugged. "You'd need to talk to your husband about that. But I *can* tell you that Medicine Horse has now brought David through for you."

"Oh, lovely. Thanks."

She looked around, frustrated that all she could see were the purple draperies, and so closed her eyes briefly and reached out mentally to the small boy she yearned for.

"He hears you. *He* wishes you could hear him speak too."

Karen jumped at the sound of Rae's voice and stared at her unblinkingly.

"How on earth do you know what I was thinking about?"

Rae laughed.

"I don't, but David does. David can read your thoughts all the while Medicine Horse is with me."

"Bloody hell!" Karen exhaled forcefully. "I'd better be careful then!"

Rae chuckled.

"Think of another question, and he'll answer it."

Karen's expression became pensive.

Did Mick really leave you to die on the moor?

The clock seemed to tick louder in the ensuing silence. Max sat up and Karen noticed his eyes following something or someone unseen. The dog gave one bark and settled down again in his basket.

"Max sees what I see." Rae patted the Alsatian's head. "David tells me that yes, Mick left him to die."

Karen's heart sank at the medium's words.

"I can't understand it." She shook her head. "It's not like Mick at all.

Rae gave a sympathetic smile.

"I'm sorry, but I cannot take back what Spirit tell me. I'm just an intermediary vessel and have no control over what is said and done."

"I see." Karen sighed. "Can David suggest anything that might be used as proof?"

"Just his words, I'm afraid." Rae replied. "It's David's word against Mick's."

Karen shrugged.

"Then we're no further forward, are we?"

Rae took a sip of water.

"Talk to your husband. Try and find a way forward."

"What's the point?" Karen leaned back in her chair and closed her eyes. "He'll deny it again. We're at an impasse. What does Medicine Horse say?"

Rae was quiet for a moment before replying.

"He lets David come through to me and keeps out any evil spirits. He doesn't have any influence over what your son says."

What had she hoped to gain from this meeting? Karen, disappointed, sat up and gathered her bag and coat together. There was nothing else for it but to talk to Mick.

CHAPTER 13 – KAREN

The house had become a shit-tip. Karen stood stupefied at the sight of mouldering dishes that Mick had left to fester on the kitchen table. On checking the fridge, an unpleasant fug of rotting food permeated her nostrils when she opened the door. The washing machine, full of damp clothes, emitted an odour that could only be trumped by a house containing many wet dogs.

Working quickly she threw his wet clothes in the tumble drier, then emptied the fridge of furry food before loading the dishwasher. While the crockery rattled in its pre-wash, she filled a bucket with hot soapy water and wiped down the surfaces. She found her mop, dry and still where she had previously left it, and cleaned the food encrusted lino. Face furrowed in grim determination, she was vacuuming the hall carpet when she heard his key turn in the lock.

His face registered a modicum of surprise. Karen turned off the vacuum cleaner and sighed.

"This place is in a bloody state! I can't believe you've let it go downhill so much!"

"To what do I owe the pleasure?" Mick threw his keys on the telephone table. "Have you come here to accuse me of sodomising next door's toddler?"

Karen gave him a thin smile.

"Give me time, and I might. I've come to talk about the mess we're in, but seeing as you were out I thought I'd try and clean up a bit."

"I like it as it is." Mick pushed past her into the kitchen. "I don't have to worry about getting anything dirty and being given a bollocking."

She switched the vacuum on again and pushed its nozzle angrily into the skirting boards as she worked, noticing with delight how it made little indentations in Mick's recent coat of gloss paint.

"Give it up!"

His voice shouting at her from behind brought her up short. She switched off the cleaner and turned to face him.

"Come and have a cup of tea, for Christ's sake."

Karen wiped her sweaty brow with the back of her hand and followed Mick into the kitchen, grateful for the noise of the dishwasher and tumble drier which filled the silence between them. She sat down and took a sip of tea.

"Ta."

"That's the last cup." Mick shrugged and sat down opposite her. "All the rest are either broken or in the dishwasher."

"Great."

Karen took another gulp of tea and then wrinkled her nose.

"This milk's going off."

"Never mind about the milk." Mick regarded her earnestly. "What are we going to do about *us*?"

Karen pushed the cup away.

"What *is* there to do, in all reality? It's David's word against yours, and he isn't here to stand up for himself."

"Well, *I* am." Mick replied firmly. "But you won't believe *me*, instead you're eating up everything that stupid woman tells you. She's after your money! Don't you see that?"

Karen shook her head.

"She does my readings for free, as a friend. She's genuine, Mick. Even you must know that. She told me you went to see her. What did she tell you?"

"Either she's good, or she's done loads of research on us." Mick shrugged. "I'm not sure which yet. She told me something I've never even told you, but she could have trawled through newspaper cuttings or even contacted the council or something like that."

"Your birth mother came through?" Karen looked at him questioningly.

Mick slammed one fist down on the table.

"How the fuck did you know that? Did she spill the beans about everything that went on?"

Karen shook her head.

"Your mum told me years ago. I figured you'd tell me when you're ready."

Relieved to see him calming down, Karen continued.

"Thousands of kids have had bad starts in life. It's nothing to be ashamed of."

The dishwasher pinged at the end of its cycle. Mick walked over to it and took a clean cup from the top basket.

"I didn't really want to share standing over my mother's dead body aged five and waiting for her to wake up from yet another alcoholic stupor."

"Sorry." Karen took a sharp intake of breath. "Rae's the most fantastic medium. She doesn't do any research. It's a gift."

"Yeah, well. She's got it wrong this time. "Mick switched on the kettle again. "If you carry on with these accusations I'll probably end up in prison for something I didn't do, and you'll have to live with the fact that you sent me there."

Karen put her head in her hands.

"How the hell do we move forward?"

The noise of his spoon as he stirred in the usual two teaspoons of sugar irritated her beyond measure.

"Who knows?" Mick took a noisy slurp of tea. "Perhaps we'll have to see what the police come up with. This living apart thing, is it permanent?"

"I haven't yet decided." Karen replied. "I just need to get my head around it all."

CHAPTER 14 - DAVID

Life had been perfect; he had been the centre of his parents' world. Then his dad had to go and spoil it all by running off with Christine from the Exams Department. He had hated to see his mum so distraught and depressed. Nothing he tried to do could help her until Mick had come along to pick up the pieces. Then it was like he, David, wasn't there either. They'd kissed and cuddled and shut him out.

David transported himself back to that chilly day at Okehampton Fair; the noise of excited kids screaming on the rides, people running to and fro, the smell of hot dogs and candy-floss, and the shouts of the stall holders. As his nine-year-old self walked with his stepfather towards the ghost train, he felt Mick's irritation rising.

"What's making that ghost move backwards and forwards on top of the building?"

"It's probably connected to a motor." Mick sighed and lit a cigarette. "Or it might even be a real one and swoop down and carry you off in a minute."

David coughed as a plume of cigarette smoke blew in his face.

"There's no such thing as ghosts."

"What do you know?" Mick exhaled. "You think you know everything, but you know sod all."

David knew one thing; he knew he hated Mick Curtis. Mick was the reason his dad had not come back. When Mick stopped at the ticket office, David shook his head.

"I don't want to go on the ghost train."

He looked up at Mick, who was chatting to the person inside the booth. David, frightened of the darkness and what might jump out at him on the train, sidled away behind the hook-a-duck stall.

"Your mum's finished work now, David. I can take you to her if you like."

David smiled at Mr Simkins, the young trendy, bearded teacher from Junior One, as the man began to walk away quickly towards the car park.

"How did you know she was at work?" He ran to keep up with Mr Simkins, pleased to be away from Mick. "Did she tell you?"

"I spoke to her at school yesterday."

David remembered stuffy warmth inside the car, a bag of toffees, and a blanket. Over the years his brain had blocked out the worst of Mr Simkins' depraved actions, but it had taken a long, long time for his mother to pluck up enough courage to visit that medium. If only she'd seen one sooner, then David knew his revenge could have started much earlier. Mick needed to pay for ruining the relationship between his mother and father.

Thanks to his cunning plan, the seeds of suspicion had already been planted in his mother's mind. It wouldn't be long before Mick, the stepfather from hell, would be gone for good. With a bit of luck after Mick had left, his father and mother might even get back together.

For the first time in a long while David felt content in his limbo. The medium was a pushover. Perhaps it was time to raise his game a little bit more.

***

He couldn't reach his mother without getting past Medicine Horse. The six foot seven sentinel always guarded the Styx and the entrance to the Avernic gates, a formidable opponent to the nine year old boy David still wanted to remain. He knew he had to keep all thoughts of Mick's comeuppance out of his mind as he waited with his grandmother to be escorted safely through into Earth's atmosphere.

"You're quiet." Esther Seeley looked down at him. "Cat got your tongue?"

David smiled.

"I'm just excited to be able to speak to Mum."

"Not much longer to wait." Esther ruffled her grandson's head. "I might even be able to get in touch with Andrew if he's about."

"Dad never wants to speak to *me*." David complained bitterly. "I don't know why."

"Mum will be waiting, I'm sure." Esther replied soothingly. "We'll just have to hope that your dad will find us one day."

David sighed with impatience as the queue shuffled slowly forward. He turned his head away from the evil spirits convening and wailing in limbo in front of the Avernic gates on the dark side of the river, and flashed a beaming smile at Medicine Horse.

"The boat is nearly full." Medicine Horse pointed to two empty seats. "Be quick."

David helped his grandmother into the boat, before taking his seat next to her. Medicine Horse stepped onto the deck, and then gave a signal to Charon, the ferryman. The boat sped noiselessly on its way.

CHAPTER 15 – RAE

The boy had obviously been waiting a while for his mother to arrive for another reading; he seemed impatient. Rae mentally acknowledged David as he appeared with Medicine Horse in tow, and also another spirit; a woman aged around seventy.

"David's here. He says he's brought his grandmother too."

"Esther?" Karen looked to Rae for confirmation.

"Yes. Granny Esther."

However, Rae could sense something different about the boy. He seemed agitated, edgy. She tried to read Medicine Horse's expression, but the Red Indian carried on maintaining his impassive stance.

"What would you like to say to your mother, David?"

Rae's thought waves reached their target as she saw the boy let go of his grandmother's hand and walk up to where Karen sat looking hopefully about the room.

"He gave me a toffee, then put his hand inside my trousers."

Rae closed her eyes in the pregnant silence of the room, and sent out a thought message.

"Picture the scene in your mind, David. Make it real, and show me."

He did what she had hoped. The nine year old's eyes unwittingly focused on features she did not recognise; a young-looking bearded man with shoulder length dark hair. Rae was mindful of Karen's questioning gaze as she tuned in to the boy's thought waves.

"Who is that man, David?"

Straight away the boy ran towards Charon and the Avernic gates, with Esther and Medicine Horse in hot pursuit. Rae sighed and shook her head.

"I'm sorry, Karen. I don't think David wants to play today after all. However, before he ran off he, whether mistakenly or not, showed me the face of another man. I sensed from David that this man had given him a toffee before he sexually abused and killed your son."

Karen regarded Rae intently.

"Are you saying David lied or made a mistake before? Is this man instead of, or as well as, Mick?"

"I will need to speak to my spirit guide." Rae replied evenly. "I cannot get David back now unless he wants to come of his own free will."

Karen's disappointment showed in her features.

"When should I return then?"

Rae stood up.

"I'll call you. Sorry, but I need to talk to Medicine Horse."

Rae felt sympathy for her friend, who was close to tears. However, the link had temporarily broken, and there was nothing for it but to end the visit. She returned to the office after Karen had departed, closed her eyes, and sent out thought waves to her loyal spirit guide.

The old Indian appeared, arms folded, at her call.

"I am here."

Rae sighed.

"You think the same as I do, don't you?"

"Indeed." Medicine Horse inclined his head. "The boy lies for reasons of his own."

"I agree." Rae replied with some relief. "You'll have to bring him back when I know his mother will be here again. We need to find out who the man is. I assume he and his grandmother are back through the gates?"

"They are." Medicine Horse nodded. "I will speak to the boy and try to persuade him to return."

Rae smiled.

"Thank you. In the meantime I'll engage the services of a psychic artist."

***

She saw the back of Karen's head in the second row straight away as she walked down the aisle to polite applause. Her friend sat alone and silent, and somewhat apart from the others. The usual hushed anticipation descended over the hall as Rae took her place on the stage.

"Good evening everybody, and thanks to Sue for inviting me." Rae acknowledged the Women's Institute chairwoman with a nod. "It's great that so many of you have braved the weather and come out tonight. Have any of you seen me at work before?"

A few hands shot up, and Rae smiled at Karen, who had risen to her feet.

"This lady is awesome." Karen pointed a finger in the direction of the stage. "She's the most gifted medium ever!"

"Why, thank you." Rae chuckled as Karen took her seat again. "You're very kind."

Medicine Horse, arms folded, stood guard in his usual place while behind him formed an orderly line of the deceased. Rae gave a nod to the Red Indian, and the first spirit ran past and sat next to a forty something woman wearing mourning black. The woman's eyes followed her every move as Rae walked towards her.

"Your husband is here with you."

The worried lines on the woman's features disappeared, and her face broke out into a smile that Rae could only class as beatific.

"I knew he'd come through!"

"There was an accident with a hedge trimmer." Rae felt the effect of a bolt of electricity shooting through her body. "Nobody saw him until it was too late."

"Yes." The woman sighed; tears already filling her eyes. "He was only forty one. He knew the wiring was faulty."

Rae nodded.

"He's sorry for leaving you so soon, but he wants you to know that he loves you very much. When you were looking through the old photo albums yesterday, he says he was there with you."

"I felt his presence." The woman replied tearfully. "You've confirmed it for me."

Rae gently touched the woman's hand.

"May God be with you."

A round of applause sent the unlucky gardener on his way. Rae looked past Medicine Horse at the ever-growing queue, but David was nowhere to be seen. A long evening stretched before her. Karen's face was full of hope, but Rae felt a keen sense of disappointment at having to let her friend down. Only Medicine Horse could help them now or perhaps Evelyn, her psychic artist friend. She would need to set up a meeting. She sent thought waves of David to the back of the hall, but only received a curt shake of a feathered headdress.

CHAPTER 16 – MICK

The pile of unwashed dishes had increased substantially since his wife's last impromptu visit. Mick failed in his search for one more clean plate for his Chinese takeaway, and so ate distractedly from its silver foil container whilst slouched in his armchair watching TV.

A key in the lock and light footsteps up the hall caused him to look around in surprise.

"What are you doing here?"

Karen wrinkled her nose.

"I used to live here, remember? What's that smell?"

"Prawns' balls and Chow Mein."

Mick turned his attention back to the TV and shovelled more food into his mouth, recalling the days when his wife would laugh at the pun.

"We've got to talk."

Mick sighed as he picked up the TV's remote control.

"You've no idea how much a fella hates to hear those words."

He muted the sound of a newsreader and turned to face her, as she sat herself down demurely on the sofa.

"There's something you need to know."

"Oh yeah?" He sat up and regarded her with interest. "What's that?"

She fiddled with a zip on her handbag before replying.

"Rae thinks David has been lying about his murderer, but she doesn't know why. He mistakenly showed her the face of another man when he talked about the day he died."

"Huh." Mick pushed the remains of his dinner to one side. "So I'm not London's answer to the Moors' Murderers then?"

"Hopefully not."

She had even managed a smile. Mick felt a black cloud of depression lift from around his head.

"What happens about us?"

Karen shrugged.

"We take it slowly and see what happens. D'you want a cup of tea?"

Mick shook his head and got to his feet.

"I'll do it. Don't go out there. I haven't cleaned up for a while."

He sighed and followed behind her as she jumped up and made for the kitchen.

"You're living in a pigsty!"

He caught up and stood behind her as she surveyed the room, silently agreeing that sadly the kitchen was not presenting its best face.

"I haven't had much incentive to do anything lately."

"Well, I'm not cleaning it up again. If I'm to come back here and live, you're going to have to do your share of housework."

Mick strode over to the kettle.

"I did tell you to stay put in the living room, didn't I? Of course if I knew you were going to show up then I would've done something about it. It'd be great to be believed instead of you constantly thinking the worst of me. David's got between us even from beyond the grave, just as he always tried to do when he was alive."

"Now you're being ridiculous!" Karen replied, her voice rising. "He was just a little boy!"

Mick waggled a finger at her.

"He was intelligent and he wanted his dad back … he *still* wants his dad back by the sound of it. He's got through from wherever he is, and at the moment his plan's succeeding, isn't it?"

The silence confirmed her tacit agreement. Mick rinsed and dried two cups and then handed Karen a cup of tea.

"How do things stand with his dad… you know, between the two of you?"

"As far as I know, Andrew's still happily married. Ta for the tea." Karen gave Mick a nod. "I haven't seen him in years, but as you know we've always kept each other updated with address and phone number changes just in case there was any news about David, but that's all."

Mick took his tea to the kitchen table and sat down.

"So why is David acting this way?"

"Rae says there's no time as such in the Spirit world." Karen sat in a chair opposite. "As far as David's concerned Andrew and I have probably not long split up. Rae was right … you can see that now, can't you? She was acting on what David told her at that demonstration we went to. There's no way she could have known he was lying."

"I give her credit for her accuracy." Mick admitted reluctantly. "Yeah…I'll give her that. I always thought it was a load of old bollocks, as you know."

Karen took a sip of tea.

"I'm glad you found out it isn't, but it still leaves *us* in a bit of a mess. Rae phoned to ask me back to witness a psychic artist at work by the way. You can come too if you like."

"That's not a good idea." Mick shook his head. "David might come through if it's just *you* there. But what we can do together is work on *us,* and also work on who actually killed David. It certainly wasn't me, and for all we know the killer's probably still out there somewhere."

"Perhaps the psychic artist can help. "Karen replied." As for *us*, let me know when you've cleaned the place up." Karen replied. "In the meantime we also need to speak to the police and find out if they're any further forward."

Mick smiled.

"I'll stay up cleaning all fucking night if it means you'll come back home."

***

He yawned as the carriage clock in the front room chimed 4am. Mick emptied the vacuum cleaner's contents into a bin, then traipsed slowly around the house with a black sack collecting any stray rubbish that had accumulated in hard-to-find nooks and crannies. One last check of the kitchen boasted a gleaming cooker shining under the fluorescent light, an empty dishwasher and washing machine, and clear work surfaces. Mick ran one finger along a pristine skirting board, and grinned at the lack of dust. Upstairs the bathroom was cleaner than he'd ever seen it, and the bed had a fresh-smelling duvet cover, sheet and pillowcases.

He showered off the day's dirt, sent photos to Karen of each room as proof of his endeavours, and then flopped into bed exhausted.

CHAPTER 17 - RAE

"Good to see you again, Evelyn. Do come in. You haven't changed a bit!"

Evelyn, tall, willowy, and with long dark hair still falling from a centre parting, hitched her capacious bag over her shoulder and stepped into the hallway.

"You old flatterer, you." She chuckled. "How have you been, Rae?"

Rae closed the front door and ushered Evelyn along the passageway.

"Can't complain. Go through…you know where the office is. As I told you on the phone, it's an interesting little project."

"It sure is." Evelyn replied. "I'm quite excited about it."

Rae saw Karen look up with interest as her friend entered the room.

"Evelyn, this is Karen, the mother of David Nelson, who was murdered about 15 years' ago. Karen, this is my friend Evelyn who is a psychic artist. She's going to tune in to my thought waves and try and draw a picture of David's killer."

Karen stood up.

"Hi." She held out her hand, somewhat excitedly. "Pleased to meet you."

"Likewise." Evelyn clasped Karen's fingers in a firm grip. "I just hope I can help today."

"Take a seat, do. There's fruit juice or water there for you both, so just help yourselves." Rae indicated towards the coffee table. "Karen, did you remember to bring something of David's for me to hold?"

Karen nodded.

"Yes, an old school jumper. He'd worn the elbows through. I just couldn't get rid of it."

Evelyn rummaged in her bag and brought out a sketchpad and a selection of pencils, just as Rae reached forward and took the jumper in both hands.

"Karen, I'm not going to say much after this. You'll see me close my eyes as I summon Medicine Horse, who'll hopefully bring David through. If he doesn't come, I'm going to try and remember what he showed me in that split second before he realised what he'd done. Evelyn will have her eyes closed too, as it's Spirit that draws what she can see in her head. There's nothing to be alarmed about, but it's not Evelyn who will be drawing the picture."

"Okay." Karen replied, a little warily. "Good luck to both of you."

Rae gave a nod to Evelyn, who raised her right thumb. The room fell silent apart from the ticking of a clock, Rae's long regular breaths, and a frantic scraping of pencil over paper.

***

He was there, waiting. Rae signalled to her faithful guide.

"How is it with you, Medicine Horse?"

The old Indian, arms folded, nodded his head in greeting.

"David is not with Charon. He is afraid he will give away the secrets of his heart."

Rae looked across the Styx, but could see nothing behind the Avernic gates.

"Tell him he already has, and that I remember the face he showed me. Tell him I know his stepfather is not a murderer, and that his mother isn't happy he would have sent an innocent man to prison."

Medicine Horse closed his eyes in meditation, and a small figure appeared behind the gates. Rae smiled at the boy.

"Hello David."

The Styx stretched its vastness between them. David hung his head in shame.

"I'm sorry."

Rae stepped as far forward as she dared. The waters of the Styx lapped around her feet, and Medicine Horse held up one hand in alarm.

"Help me to trap the real killer, David! Show me again what he looked like so that I can get a better likeness. Did you know him?"

"It was Mr Simkins."

Rae sighed with relief.

"Who is he? Did you know him?"

The boy raised his head.

"Yes. He is a teacher at my school. He called the school to assembly after I disappeared, and told all the children to pray for me."

"David, thank you for this." Rae stepped back from the shoreline. "Thank you so much.

***

She was never aware of time passing, and always liked to look at the clock afterwards. Evelyn still scribbled furiously as she added a touch of colour to her finished picture. Rae smiled at Karen and realised that 45 minutes had evaporated in the blink of an eye.

"Okay?"

"I think so." Karen nodded. "I don't really know. Can I have a look at Evelyn's drawing, please?"

"Yes, I've finished now." Evelyn handed her work to Rae. "Is this what you saw?"

The man's dark hair touched his shoulders. The beard was full but neatly trimmed. Brown eyes stared into the depths of hell.

"Absolutely." Rae nodded vigorously. "Evie, you're remarkable as usual! Karen… do you recognise this man?"

Rae gave the drawing to Karen, watching closely for any reaction. In a trice all colour had drained from her friend's face.

"My God!" Karen put a hand to her mouth in horror. "It's one of the teachers from David's old school! I remember the long hair and beard! That's Barry Simkins!"

"Yes." Rae agreed with a nod. "That's what David told me."

"Can I have this to show the police?" Karen looked imploringly at Evelyn. "This is amazing. It's like looking at a photo of him."

"Of course." Evelyn gave a smile. "You're more than welcome to take it."

Rae held up one hand in caution.

"Karen, this is how David remembers this man. Fifteen years have gone by, and he probably looks nothing like this anymore."

"Yes, you're right." Karen nodded. "But now the police have something to go on. Hopefully they can find him and do a discreet check. I must tell Mick. I remember Mick even told me at the time that he'd bumped into the bastard at the fair, but I never thought anything of it."

Rae stood up.

"I'll come with you to the police station to verify everything, but in the meantime I'll put the kettle on. I think we could all do with a strong cup of tea."

CHAPTER 18 – BARRY

Barry Simkins looked across his desk at the student, and wished not for the first time that he could thrash the boy into next week in order to wipe the smirk off his self-satisfied face. Jardine Minor knew the ropes just as well as his older brother did; teachers could be prosecuted for using a cane, even at Swithinbank, a school previously not unused to corporal punishment.

"You'll do extra prep this evening in your free time. Mr Hudson will be on duty tonight, and will arrange it."

"Yes Sir." Jardine exhaled slowly in relief.

"Get out of my sight."

The door slammed. Receding footsteps and muted giggling only served to enrage Simkins more. Jardine Major had doubtless had his ear pressed against the wall, with mobile phone primed to call home. Simkins, hands metaphorically tied with a crushing impotence, picked up Jardine Minor's thick report file and hurled it at the door.

"Fucking bastard kid!"

Papers fluttered on the agitated air before settling. Simkins, suddenly conscious of Clare Vincent's presence in the secretaries' office, leapt up from his desk and picked up page after page containing Jardine Minor's shortcomings. A high pitched voice emanated from the next room.

"Everything okay, Barry?"

Simkins sighed.

"Just fine. I dropped something."

He threw Jardine's file onto a nearby chair and strode out into the now quiet corridor. Boys had arrived at their assigned classrooms, and the first lesson after lunch had begun. Masters' voices droned through ancient oak-panelled doors. Everything was in order, and Simkins needed to regain his headmaster's calm equilibrium which the Jardine brothers constantly sought to destroy.

He climbed Staircase 1 to the first floor. As he stepped into the corridor he faced the unwelcome sight of 14 year old Jardine Minor recumbent on a windowsill outside the chemistry lab.

"Stand up, boy! Why aren't you in your lesson?"

The boy stared him out and got to his feet with a purposeful and agonising slowness.

"Mr Kent said I'd soon do something to disrupt the lesson, so he told me to stand outside before the lesson even started."

Simkins decided not to give Jardine the satisfaction of knowing he had pushed the chemistry master *and* the headmaster to the limits of their endurance. He took a firm grip on the boy's blazer.

"Come with me. It's time we sorted out your tiresome behaviour once and for all."

"But I haven't done anything, Sir!" Jardine Minor protested indignantly. "Mr Kent sent me out for no reason!"

"Ah, but Mr Kent is correct. You *would* have done something sooner or later, wouldn't you?" Simkins replied drily. "We're going out into the grounds to have a little talk."

"I've done nothing! It's not my fault! It's Mr Kent, Sir – he sent me out!"

Jardine's cat-like gaze and blustery bravado irritated him more than he would ever admit. A red hot rage descended over Simkins' powers of reason as he marched the boy down Staircase 1. Jardine had been a thorn in his side for three years, and his brother for even longer. It was time to put an end to teenage insubordination on an industrial scale.

Simkins, still holding onto Jardine Minor, walked quickly to the end of the downstairs corridor and slipped out through a fire door exit. Well-tended grounds stretched before them; a newly mown rugby pitch, tennis courts, an outdoor swimming pool, and on the other side of a fence lay two miles of dense National Trust forestry. Looking up, he noticed with approval how all south-facing classroom blinds were drawn against the afternoon sun as, nursing a growing erection, he made his way with the boy towards the cover of woodland. There was no going back now.

Just in time he noticed the boy fumbling in his pocket and then his thumb on the phones' keyboard.

"You won't need that where we're going." He took a firm hold on the back of the boy's collar, and with his free hand grabbed Jardine's phone. "Walk faster."

Simkins felt the warmth of the boy's neck under his collar as he dodged a kick from Jardine's boot. He hadn't felt so alive since the night of the Okehampton fair in 2004. A similar excitement had suffused his being back then which could not be ignored, and release had only come with David Nelson's death. Now it was happening again. The boy struggled to extricate himself. Simkins threw caution to the wind and marched onward towards the trees, panting slightly on arrival at the chest-high wooden fence separating Swithinbank's grounds from National Trust land.

"Climb over and stand still."

In a trice Jardine Minor had vaulted the fence and hit the ground running. Incensed, Simkins hauled himself over the barrier and set off in hot pursuit.

"Come back here, you little shit!"

He'd never had cause to venture any further than the fence. He listened carefully as Jardine's feet beat out a tattoo on the forest floor, with cracked twigs and ruffled leaves giving welcome clues to the boy's location. Simkins, breathing hard, dodged treacherous tree roots and pushed quickly past low hanging branches, unwilling to admit his middle-aged muscles could not outrun the 14 year old's whippet-like body. When he thought his chest might explode, he ceased running and stooped over to catch his breath.

The forest was alive with birds twittering their messages above. The avian chorus and Simkins' laboured breathing easily masked the sound of a boot connecting with his testicles from behind, which caused his knees to buckle as he crashed to the floor in agony.

"You fuckin…!"

A large branch applied with force arrested any further speech. Jardine, sweat pouring from his brow, noticed how a new dent had appeared on the back of Simkins' head. He threw the branch as far as he could into the undergrowth, and hurriedly retraced his steps to the school building. After sluicing his hands and face, he took up a recumbent position upon the window sill next to the chemistry lab. As his classmates exited the lesson, he saved his best sneer for Professor Hudson while managing to hide his dismay as he reached into an empty pocket.

CHAPTER 19 – MICK

Mick sighed with irritation. The vacuum cleaner bag was full, and he'd forgotten to order another box online. His wife was due to take up residence in the spare room at any moment and he knew her personality so well; she would be checking under the bed for fur balls.

The house phone rang. Mick switched off the vacuum cleaner and picked up the extension on the upstairs landing.

"Yeah?"

A male replied, strangely familiar.

"Mr Curtis?"

"That's right."

"This is DI Ken Richardson."

"Oh."

Richardson cleared his throat.

"Er… there's no easy way to say this, but we need you or your wife to travel back up here to the station. I know it's a long way from London, but there's been new developments in David's case."

"Am I going to be arrested again as soon as I get there?"

"No." DI Richardson coughed again. "Your wife had given us a picture of David at the start of all this, and as you know, Mrs Cordelle's psychic artist came up with a face that your wife recognised as Barry Simkins, David's teacher. Simkins was found dead recently, and we've just managed to unlock his computer with a little bit of help."

"And…" Mick replied slowly.

"And… amongst thousands of unsettling images there are pictures on the hard drive that he'd taken of what we think is David's body. We need you or your wife to make an identification. Unfortunately I am not allowed to email the photos to you. They must stay on the computer."

Mick felt his stomach lurch.

"Does Karen know about this?"

"Not yet." Richardson replied. "But I'll leave it to you to tell her. Will you come?"

"Sure." Mick agreed with a sigh. "I won't say anything to Karen though until I've seen the photos. I'll grab an overnight bag and will be with you in the morning."

***

Mick drummed his fingers impatiently on the steering wheel at the sight of three lanes of red tail lights in his vision. His mobile vibrated on the passenger seat, as he brought the car to a halt. Karen's name flashed on the display screen and her voice echoed in his ear as soon as he accepted the call.

"Are you avoiding me? I'm at home now. You haven't emptied the vacuum cleaner bag."

"There aren't any more." He rolled his eyes. "And no, I'm not avoiding you. I'll be back tomorrow at some point."

He knew her female intuition would not be happy with his reply.

"Where are you?"

"I'm staying over at Steve's. We're going for a beer and a curry."

"Well… you knew I was coming back today."

She sounded petulant. He hated himself for the lie.

"Someone at work is leaving. It's a bit of a party. I don't want to come home rat-arsed and be in your bad books straight away."

"Oh."

The queue of traffic on the M5 began to inch forward, and he could now see signs for the A38.

"Got to go. See you tomorrow."

He ended the call abruptly with a mental picture of the expression on her face. When he reached Ashburton he rang the bell of the Agaric tearooms, and was shown to a predominantly red room containing a surprisingly long Victorian gentleman's bath with original claw feet. He filled it to the brim and soaked away his stiff muscles, feeling a little apprehensive about the following day.

***

"Thanks for coming back at short notice."

Mick nodded to DI Richardson, who ushered him into the interview room he now recognised.

"There's no way to pretty up the images I'm afraid." Richardson pulled out a chair and switched on the computer. "Take a seat. I've already got some coffee organised."

"Cheers." Mick looked at the screen as it booted up. "Will this take long?"

"No time at all." Richardson replied curtly. "Here's one which shows the face better. You don't need to see the rest."

Mick's heart beat a fast rhythm in his chest, and his mouth felt dry. Unwillingly he focused on David, neck broken and body naked as he lay spread-eagled on empty moorland next to his favourite football shirt. The boy's eyes were still open, opaque in death. Mick looked away.

"It's David. I saw that fucker Simkins at the fair on the day he took David. If only I'd known what he was going to do."

He felt relieved he had risen late and hadn't had time for

breakfast. A constable entered with a tray containing two steaming cups.

"Get that down you." Richardson pushed a cup towards Mick. "You're free to go as soon as you like."

Mick took a long swig of coffee.

"What will you do now?"

Richardson switched off the monitor.

"There are emails to and from the low life he was sharing photos with. Thanks to Simkins' computer we'll be able to trace who these people are and arrest them. It's too late for David unfortunately, but hopefully some other kids might be spared."

"I hope so." Mick stood up. "Good luck."

He felt sick. He raced towards the nearest lavatory and retched until his stomach was empty.

CHAPTER 20 – ANDREW NELSON

It took a few moments for his brain to recognise the man depicted on page 8 of the newspaper.

"Look at that!" Andrew shook his head in disbelief. "Chris, come and see this!"

He held up the page as his wife, now curious, came over towards him.

"Who is it?" She followed the direction of his finger and shrugged. "I don't know him."

"He was a teacher at David's school." Andrew did a quick double take to make sure. "Older here, but still the same chap. Looks like he's come to a bit of a sticky end."

"Found in land surrounding Swithinbank School." Christine Nelson read on. "Did David go to a private school then?"

"No, more's the pity." Andrew shook his head. "Simkins must have been promoted since David's time."

Christine finished reading the article and turned to Andrew.

"Perhaps tell Karen? She won't get this local rag in London, unless it's in the national papers of course."

"I'll post it to her." Andrew agreed with a nod. "She'll be as surprised as I am."

He read the rest of the column, noting how a National Trust

groundsman had discovered the body after it had lain in a forest clearing for at least a fortnight, and that the cause of death had been a fractured skull. Andrew cut carefully around the picture and article, popped it into an envelope, and after posting thought nothing more about it.

When the phone rang two days' later he was surprised to hear his ex-wife's voice.

"Andrew – thanks for that article. It made my day."

"Why?" Andrew gave a wry laugh. "Did you want him dead?"

"Have the police not been in touch? I thought they would have done. Sorry, I should have told you. He's the shitbag who murdered David!"

An unwelcome red fury coursed through his veins. He flexed the fingers of his free hand, which had involuntarily clenched into a fist.

"How did they find out after all this time?"

There was a moment's hesitation at the other end of the line.

"There's no out-and-out proof, but what's been found is good enough. I managed to find a medium who even convinced the police. Keys to Simkins' house were in his pocket, along with a phone belonging to one of the students. When police went to his house they found thousands of child porn images on his computer. He'd even uploaded pictures he'd taken of David's body. Mick had to identify David from a photo – He knew I wouldn't have been able to do it."

"Christ." Andrew whistled softly. "Sorry Karen. I should have been there. How's Mick?"

"Shaken up. We're trying to get our lives back together. We only had proof the other day. It's all been a bit of a rollercoaster ride."

"I know I've been out of the loop for years." Andrew replied softly. "If there's anything else needs doing, just let me know."

"Cheers. Speak to you soon."

The line went dead. Andrew felt tears well up as he tried but failed to imagine his son's final agonising moments.

***

It seemed the right thing to do. Andrew stood on the doorstep of 42 Crossleys Street and rang the bell, noticing with relief how Mick's work van was not parked on the driveway.

"Hi Andrew. Come in." Karen smiled at him. "How's Christine?"

He had not been to the house in years. He noticed a faint smell of fresh gloss paint.

"She's fine. She sends her regards."

He saw new lines around her eyes that had not been there the last time he'd seen her. As he followed her into the front room, he admitted to himself why he had kept his distance; he did not want to be constantly reminded of his dead son.

"Can I get you some tea, or do you still prefer coffee?"

He smiled.

"Christine makes me drink green tea. It tasted like pond water at first, but I'm used to it now. It'll be a relief though to have some coffee."

While she was gone he took a chance to look around the room. Pictures of his son adorned the walls, and a large photo of David stood in a frame on a shelf above the TV. He'd forgotten how much the boy resembled himself at the same age. There were wedding photos of Karen and Mick, as was only proper. A fleeting thought crossed his mind as to how he compared to Mick in bed.

"Here you are." Karen breezed into the room and handed him a full cup. "I tried green tea once, but couldn't get on with it either."

He took the cup from her and sipped the welcome brew.

"Mick won't mind me coming here?"

"Not at all. He'll be home from work soon. I'm on a night shift tonight, so I don't need to leave until about seven thirty."

"Okay." Andrew nodded. "I just wanted to help in any way I can, and of course find out more about what's been going on. It's funny. We're still living in Exeter, but it's you the police contacted, two hundred miles away."

Karen shrugged.

"Well, *we* got in touch with *them* first – myself and Rae Cordelle, the medium who found David. I only wish I'd sought her out years ago. She's amazing."

"That's all a load of old bollocks, isn't it?" Andrew drained his cup and sat back in the armchair. "Isn't it just another way to extort money?"

"Maybe with some of them, but not Rae. David comes over when she's here. You ought to see her work before you go home. In fact, you *must*." Karen picked up her mobile phone from the coffee table. "I'll see if she's free. She doesn't even charge me."

He watched his ex-wife talking animatedly with somebody who could allegedly bring his son back from the dead. It didn't seem possible, and Andrew decided to go along with it, but inwardly remain highly censorious.

EPILOGUE

Richardson pulled up at an imposing outer gate and pressed the intercom.

"It's Detective Inspector Richardson. I have an appointment for ten o'clock."

The gate swung open of its own accord. As Richardson brought his car to a halt, the figure of a well-dressed man appeared at the front porch.

"'Morning." Richardson opened the driver door and stepped out. "Lloyd Jardine?"

"That's right." Jardine looked at Richardson suspiciously. "My son Lester is waiting for you in the study, but he doesn't know anything apart from what he's already told me."

Richardson entered a large mock-Tudor hallway and followed Jardine to a downstairs annexe where Lester Jardine sat nonchalantly in a room laden with books. Richardson wrinkled his nose at the faint aroma of cigar smoke.

"Sorry to disturb your school holidays, Lester."

Jardine Minor regarded Richardson impassively.

"I don't really know much."

"It's okay. I just want to speak to you, as we're also investigating another case which Mr Simkins' might have had something to do with."

"Yeah?" Lester sat up straighter. "What case?"

Richardson smiled.

"I'm not at liberty to say, but what I'd like to know is why Mr Simkins had your phone in his pocket at the time of his death."

He noticed the boy slump back against the chair with disinterest.

"He took it away from me. I looked at a message in the French lesson. Mr Moore reported me, and Mr Simkins took it away for the day."

Jardine made a 'tut' of annoyance.

"Lester, you're supposed to switch your phone off in lessons."

"I know, Dad." Lester sighed. "Sorry."

Richardson hid his disappointment.

"Had you tried to phone nine nine nine at all?"

"No." Lester shrugged. "Why would I want to do that? Mr Simkins might have tried though, if he was in trouble."

It was a plausible explanation. Richardson looked at his watch.

"Sorry to keep you. I just needed Lester to help clear up the issue with the mobile phone.

He was aware of a sigh as the boy gave a smirk and relaxed further into the chair. Something bothered him, but he couldn't put a finger on exactly what it was.

***

Now it was time; he had decided to pay the ferryman. David stepped into the boat with Medicine Horse and nodded to Charon.

"I will pay on my return."

The gargoyle jumped up and down with glee. Medicine Horse held up one hand.

"If you pay, you will not be able to travel again beyond the gates."

"I know." David agreed. "But my time on Earth is done. However, I must make one last visit across the Styx."

A queue formed to board the boat. David looked over his shoulder towards Barry Simkins, who wailed in anguish as he pummelled the Avernic gates in vain.

"Where will he go?" David turned to Medicine Horse. "Will you let him through?"

"No. He must atone for his sins. His journey to salvation will be long and arduous."

David did not press the issue. The boat, now full, glided silently across the Styx, and David saw the purple drapes of the medium's office come into view.

"I can see Mum and Dad!" David shouted excitedly. "They're together!"

"What you see is not necessarily the truth." Medicine Horse replied. "Exercise caution."

"I don't care." David stood up impatiently. "They've given me what I want."

When the boat docked he pushed past Medicine Horse and ran to stand grinning in-between his parents, who sat side by side.

"Hello Mum! Hello Dad!" David threw an arm around their necks. "I'm so glad to see both of you!"

He felt disappointed at their lack of response. However, he relaxed as Rae Cordelle shot him a beaming smile.

"Hello David. What would you like to say to your parents?"

"Tell them I'm so pleased to see them here together. Tell them Mr Simkins cannot get through the gates. And tell them I love them and that I'm sorry what I did to Mick. I wanted Mum and Dad to get back together, but I didn't realise how much time had gone past. I know now that they're just good friends. Oh, and tell Dad I know all about his heart scare. The stent will serve him well for years to come. His wife does a good job in keeping him off the sugar. Mick loves Mum I know, and in time she will trust him again."

He saw his mother smile and his father look around the room in amazement.

"Wow…nobody knows about my stent except Christine!"

Rae laughed.

"You can't keep secrets from Spirit."

David felt as though he could burst with love. However, he knew his journey on the earth plane was done and that he had to move on. It was time to pay the ferryman.

THE END

If you have enjoyed this novella, you may like 'Partners in Time' a paranormal romance also by Stevie Turner.